Please renew or return items by the date
shown on your receipt

www.hertsdirect.org/libraries

Renewals and   0300 123 4049
enquiries:

Textphone for hearing   0300 123 4041
or speech impaired

Hertfordshire

Raintree is an imprint of Capstone Global Library Limited, a company incorporated in England and Wales having its registered office at 7 Pilgrim Street, London, EC4V 6LB – Registered company number: 6695582

www.raintreepublishers.co.uk
myorders@raintreepublishers.co.uk

Text © 2014 by Picture Window Books
First published in the United Kingdom in paperback in 2014
The moral rights of the proprietor have been asserted.

Designers: Heather Kindseth Wutschke, Kristi Carlson and Philippa Jenkins
Editor: Catherine Veitch
Originated by Capstone Global Library Ltd
Printed and bound in China

ISBN 978 1 406 28045 6 (paperback)
18 17 16 15 14
10 9 8 7 6 5 4 3 2 1

British Library Cataloguing in Publication Data
A full catalogue record for this book is available
from the British Library.

Contents

Chapter 1
Poppy's great idea

Poppy plopped down on the door step. Her best friend, Millie, plopped down next to her.

"I'm bored," Poppy said.

"Me too," said Millie.

They had to play outside until dinner. Poppy was annoyed.

"I wish we could just stay inside and watch television," Poppy said.

"This village needs more excitement," Millie said. "There's nothing to do."

"I watched a new TV show last night. It was called *Get Up and Move*. Children would go on stage and show their talents," Poppy said.

"What's a talent?" Millie asked.

"It's something amazing that you can do well. One girl could hula-hoop with four hoops!" Poppy said.

"Wow!" Millie said.

Poppy had an idea. "We should have a talent show for all the children in the village!"

Millie nodded. "That's a great idea!"

Chapter 2

What's your talent?

Poppy and Millie were excited

about the talent show. It was going to

be on Saturday in Poppy's garden.

They spent the whole week getting ready. They called all their friends. They made tickets for all the parents. They were also going to have snacks, which made Poppy extra excited.

"My aunt from America is going to make ants on a log," Millie said.

"Yuck! I'm not eating ants!" Poppy said.

Millie laughed. "Not real ants, silly! It's raisins and peanut butter on celery. It's yummy!"

"Nick, what is your talent?" Poppy asked her older brother as he walked by her room.

Nick said, "I'm going to see how many times I can bounce a football on my feet."

"What's your talent, Millie?"
Poppy asked.

"I'm going to do a dance
routine," Millie said. She twirled
around.

"You are a really
good dancer,"
Poppy said.

Then she thought
of the other children.
They all had really
cool talents.

James was going to do karate.

Eva was going to do backflips.

Jacob was going to do tricks on

his bike.

"This is going to be a great show!"

Poppy said with a big smile.

"What is your talent, Poppy?"

Millie asked.

Poppy stopped smiling. "My talent?"

Poppy had been so busy planning the show, she had forgotten to work on her own talent!

Poppy knew she was a good reader. She was good at video games, too. But neither of these things were that interesting.

"You do have a talent, don't you?" Millie asked.

"Of course," Poppy lied. But she wasn't sure at all.

Chapter 3
Show time!

It was the morning of the talent show. Millie and Poppy were getting the garden ready.

"What is your talent anyway?" asked Millie.

"It's a secret," Poppy said.

They began picking up the toys from the garden. Poppy saw the skipping rope and had a great idea.

"I have to go and do something. I'll be back soon!" Poppy cried.

"Hurry back," Millie said. "I'll try to finish setting up."

"Thank you," Poppy said as she grabbed the skipping rope.

Poppy used to skip all the time. She couldn't even remember why she had stopped!

She practised all of her favourite tricks. She tripped over the rope a few times. But she kept practising. She knew she could do it.

By the time the show started, Poppy was ready.

When it was her turn, Poppy did every trick she knew. The crowd cheered with every move. Poppy felt proud and tired.

After the show, Poppy learned

something else. She liked to eat ants!

Well, ants on a log, anyway.

"Who knew ants could be so

yummy?" Poppy said to Millie.

Millie laughed and finished her

tasty snack.

"Now that the talent show is over, what are we going to do tomorrow?" Millie asked.

"I'm not sure, but I'll think of something," said Poppy. "And it will be amazing."

"It always is," agreed Millie.

Poppy's new words

I learned so many new words today! I wrote them down so that I could use them again.

annoyed feel angry or frustrated

plan work out how to do something

plop fall

practise do something again and again so that you get better at it

routine pattern of doing things

talent natural ability or skill

Poppy's thoughts

After the big talent show, I had some time to think. Here are some of my questions and thoughts from the day.

1. Would you want to be part of a talent show? Why or why not?

2. How do you think I felt when I realized I didn't have a talent? Are there any clues in the pictures?

3. I finally found a talent. What's your talent? Talk about it.

4. Write a story for a newspaper about our village talent show.

Ants on a Log

I can't believe I ate ants! (I know they weren't really ants, but it's fun to say.) Here's the recipe:

What you need:

- 1 celery stick
- peanut butter
- raisins
- butter knife

Ask an adult for help

What you do:

1. Wash and dry the celery. Cut it in half.

2. Use the butter knife to spread one big spoonful of peanut butter onto each celery stick.

3. Put 10–15 raisins on top of the peanut butter and enjoy!

Your talent

I found my talent. What's yours? Here are some talents for you to try. Have fun!

- hula-hoop

- skip

- sing

- do cartwheels or somersaults

- dance (spin, twirl, jump)

- dribble a football

- put on a magic show

- throw and catch

- see how many push-ups or jumping jacks you can do in one minute

About the author

Michele Jakubowski grew up in Chicago, United States of America (USA). She has the teachers in her life to thank for her love of reading and writing. While writing has always been a passion for Michele, she believes it is the books she has read over the years, and the teachers who introduced them, that have made her the storyteller she is today. Michele lives in Ohio, USA, with her husband, John, and their children, Jack and Mia.

About the illustrator

Erica-Jane Waters grew up in the beautiful Northern Irish countryside, where her imagination was ignited by the local folklore and fairy tales. She now lives in Oxfordshire with her young family. Erica writes and illustrates children's books and creates art for magazines, greeting cards and various other projects.